For elementary schoolteachers everywhere,
and for my own whom I clearly remember some
fifty years later:

Miss Kindevarder, Mrs. Miller, Mrs. Sarasohn,
Mrs. Vork, Miss Kelly, Miss Benson, Mrs. Sawyer,
Mrs. Jampole, Mrs. Welter, Mr. Rose

And for Albert Cullum, master teacher, who gave
me the confidence to find new ways to encourage
children to write their own stories

—H.M.Z.

Text copyright © 2004 by Harriet Ziefert
Illustrations copyright © 2004 by Amanda Haley
All rights reserved. CIP Data is available.
Published in the United States 2004 by
Blue Apple Books
515 Valley Street, Maplewood, N.J. 07040
www.blueapplebooks.com
Distributed in the U.S. by Chronicle Books

First Edition
Printed in China
ISBN: 1-59354-056-6
1 3 5 7 9 10 8 6 4 2

Schools Have
Learn

Harriet Ziefert

pictures by Amanda Haley

 Blue Apple Books

Beds
have
jumps.

Cereal has lumps.

Good-byes
have
hugs.

Backpacks have lugs.

Kids have sing.

ring ring ring

School bells
have
ring.

Lines have push.

Monitors have shush!

Desks have books.

Coats have hooks.

Teachers
have
looks.

Blackboards have chalk.

Groups
have
talk.

Students have voices.
Kids have choices.

Hands have raises.

Excellent!

Teachers
have
praises.

History has facts.

Math has subtracts.

Geometry has lines.

Multiplication tables have nines.

Schools have learn.

Books have return.

Readers have smarts.
Libraries have carts.

Fiction has tales.
Nonfiction has whales.

Noontime
has
lunches.

Celery has crunches.
Grapes have bunches.

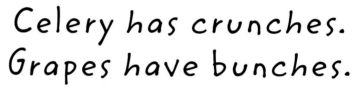

Sandwiches have bites.

Kids
have
fights.

Exits
have
signs.

Fire drills have lines.

Gyms have balls.

Legs have falls.

Hands
have
holds.

Noses have colds.

Voices have throats.
Music has notes.

Drums have beat.
Taps have feet.

Paints have drips.
Papier-mâché has strips.

Biology has plants.

Zoology has ants.

Principals
have
gazes.

Workbooks have mazes.

Words have vowels.

Rule:
i before e, except after C, or when followed by "gh" as in neighbor and Weigh.

Spellers have scowls.

Teachers have rules.

No Candy
No gum
No bare feet
No cell phones
No tape recorders

Custodians have tools.

Erasers have rub.
Pencils have stub.

Computers have bytes.

The WEB has sites.

Eyes have glasses.
Balloons have gases.

Students have rights.
Homework has nights.

Friends have greets.
Auditoriums have seats.

Classes have plays.

Actors have ways...

Teachers have bouquets!